KV-510-097

To

Robert and
Rory Stephens

'Mum, I want a dog,' said Rory.
'All the boys at school have dogs.'

'I'll see,' said Mum.

'I want a dog, too,' said Robert.
'I want a St Bernard.'

'That's too big,' said Mum.

‘I don’t want a St Bernard,’ said Rory. ‘I want a Siberian Husky.’

'That's too fierce,' said Mum.

Next Morning

'Mum, I really do want a dog,'
said Rory.
'Me too,' said Robert.

'I'll think about it,' said Mum. 'But not a Siberian Husky. Now, where did I put my shopping list?'

'We'll get a St Bernard, then,' said Robert.

'No, not a St Bernard either,' said Mum. 'I told you before. That's too big.'

'Mum, I want a dog,' said Rory.
'I want a Siberian Husky.'

'Rory, I told you! We're not getting a Siberian Husky.'

'Well then, what about an Irish Wolfhound,' said Rory.

'You would never be able to hold it,' said Mum. 'It would pull you down the road.'

'I could go on my skateboard,' said Rory.

'Don't be silly, Rory,' said Mum.

'Mum, when *are* you going to think about a dog?' said Robert. 'When you're in bed and asleep,' said Mum.

Next Day

'Come on, Rory and Robert. Get in the car. I've got a present for you at home,' said Mum.

'I bet it's a dog!' said Robert.

'Well, yes, it is,' said Mum.

‘I hope it’s a German Shepherd,’ said Robert.

'Or a Great Dane,' said Rory.
'Just wait and see,' said Mum.

'Is that it?' said Rory.
'Cool!' said Robert.

Two Days Later

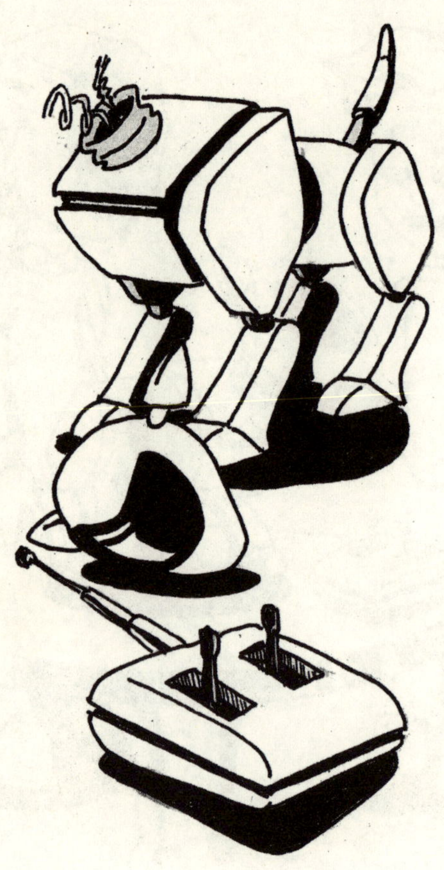

'Rory broke it,' said Robert.

'I didn't want it anyway,' said Rory. 'I want a real dog. I want a Siberian Husky.'

A Week Later

'The gold fish is for Robert and the striped fish is for Rory.'

‘My one is better than your one,’ said Rory.

'No, it's not,' said Robert.

'Mum, we don't want toys and we don't want fish,' said Rory. 'We want a dog.'

'I'll think about it when we come back from holiday,' said Mum.

On Holiday

'Look at that Afghan hound,' said Robert. 'I'd like a dog like that when we get back home.'

'Too much hair,' said Mum.

'Dad, please can we have a dog?' said Rory. 'We'd really love a dog.'

'I'll think about it,' said Dad. 'Let's just enjoy our last day on holidays.'

Back Home

'Let's go and see Aunt Ann,' said Mum. 'She will want to know all about our holidays.'

'Oh, no,' said Rory. 'Boring!'
'But I thought you two boys enjoyed playing with her dog,' said Mum.

'Look, our dog has had puppies,' said Aunt Ann. 'They all have homes except this black fellow.'

'Cute, aren't they?' said Robert.

'Well,' said Rory as he patted the mother dog. 'You're not exactly a Siberian Husky, are you? But you are cute.'

'I really like the little black fellow,' said Robert.
'He's sweet, isn't he,' said Aunt Ann.

'I like the little black fellow too,' said Rory.

'Oh, Mum, please,' said the boys.
'Oh, all right, then,' said Mum.

'Let's hope that keeps them quiet,'
said Mum to Aunt Ann.

'When he's a bit bigger we'll take him for walks in the wood every day,' said Robert to Rory. 'Yeah,' said Rory. 'That will be cool!'